One In a Dogzillion

BY MELODY POILVEZ

ILLUSTRATED BY FRANK TENEDORA

DEDICATION

For Mom and Sweets,

Thank you for always believing in me. I love you with all my heart. – MP

For Maia and Zander, my heart and soul. – FT

Have you ever met Max the world's biggest dog?

He eats more than a dinosaur and snores like a hog.

He has the breath of a dragon and the bark of a beast,

But there is not a mean bone in his body, not in the least!

This giant has soft chocolate brown eyes.

He loves to eat apple, cherry, and blueberry pies.

Max has fur that is a shiny black and gold

As well as huge claws that get bigger when he's cold.

His large ears can hear everything far and nearby.

He even hears when ants say hello and goodbye!

Max has big white teeth sharp like a nail,

And a fluffy tail that's as long as a whale.

4

Max's best friend is a tiny cat! Pepper is her name.

Together they laugh and play every possible game.

Pepper the cat is feisty and a little bossy, but that's okay,

Max does not mind because they have so much fun when they play.

Max dreams about flying through the clouds upside down,

While Pepper pretends to fly like a super hero over the town.

They also cuddle together when taking a nap

Even though Pepper is smaller than a baseball cap.

Max and Pepper live in a little town

That once upon a time made Max frown.

Max did not feel liked or accepted from the first day

As everyone who saw Max ran the other way.

"He's a monster! Run away!" they would say.

They called him Dogzilla and told him to move far away.

Animals hid from Max in their homes, in trees, even in the hay.

"He looks scary and must be mean" they would scream

Afraid Max would eat them up like a scoop of ice cream.

Little did they know that they were wrong in every way.

Deep down inside, Max is a teddy bear who just wants to play.

Those mean words made Max sad,

But this sweet boy did not get angry or mad.

Max knew being bigger, meant in no way that he was bad.

He liked himself just as he was inside out, and of that, he was glad.

No matter how hurtful villagers were, Max stayed true to himself.

He could not change his ears, nose, and legs to be the size of an elf!

One day, the villagers hatched a plan and drew it on a map.

It was a plan for which they even built a trap.

They wanted to catch the scary looking beast,

Even though they did not know him in the least.

The stories they made up about Max caused everyone alarm.

Yet, to no one he had done any harm.

Pepper was upset with the way everyone talked about her best friend.

To this nonsense, she decided to put an end!

In all her fluffiness, Pepper strolled down to City Hall

With her head held up high and walking tall.

Only a bossy cat like Pepper could fix this mess.

For the special event, she even wore a pink dress!

This brave cat pranced up to the large crowd.

She took a deep breath, and then spoke these very words aloud:

"Villagers you have been silly and mean.

You judged my friend Max based only on what you have seen.

Now it is time for you to open your ears and be wise.

Stop being afraid and learn about Max beyond his size.

Max is a gentle dog who lets me take his toys and bed.

He always shares and gives me big slobbery kisses on the head.

Max might not always behave,

But like a hero, he is brave.

He may burp and he may fart,

But he has a giant loving heart.

He howls along with fire truck sirens as if they were songs,

And it's right here in our town that he belongs!

I love this giant dog in every way

No matter what some rude people might say!

You see, we all have a heart,

But it's how we use it that truly sets us apart.

It's what is on the inside that matters most.

Not silly things like size, color, or if you cut the crust off of your toast.

Be kind, loving, caring, respectful, and honest.

Max is, and those qualities make him the best.

It does not matter how you look, what you wear, or what you eat.

Max will be your friend even if you eat worms and have stinky feet."

24

Pepper had said everything she came to say,

So she turned her tiny paws around and went on her way.

She hoped her speech would stop everyone from being rude.

All of this fighting was putting her in an awful bad mood.

Pepper was excited to return to her normal day,

Where she could nap, take selfies with her best friend Max, and play.

The villagers were speechless. What could they say?

They promised to start thinking first with their hearts, that very same day.

They all wondered what they could do to fix their mistake.

A small brown rabbit promised to bake Max a cake.

The fox held up a pen and offered to write Max a song.

The bee said she could make enough honey to last Max all year long.

An owl in the back spoke: "telling Max we are sorry is a good start,

Let's hope he forgives us with his great big giant heart."

The owl was right, an honest "I am sorry" is what they needed to say.

Those three magic words can go a very long way!

Meanwhile, to avoid being seen, Max wore a disguise.

However, those big wigs and sunglasses only work for spies.

So when everyone recognized Max, it was no surprise,

But when villagers came to him smiling, Max could not believe his eyes!

No bullying, no shouting, no name-calling, and no attacks!

They all looked at the gentle giant and said: "we are sorry Max."

Max was so happy that everyone was nice.

Every single villager hugged him, even the mice!

The villagers realized that Max was no danger at all.

He protected them from everything big and small.

Max's long wagging tail fanned cool air when it was hot,

And his long claws were perfect to undo any knot.

Some villagers stood under him in the rain to stay dry.

Max even carried home birds that could not fly.

Upon seeing these changes, Pepper was so pleased she began to purr.

After all, peace would have never been found if not for her!

Pepper could now take a nap and relax,

Happy and proud she was able help her best friend Max!

Now the villagers call Max by a new nickname.

This one is kind, and not at all lame.

They call him "Goodzilla"

Which Max likes even more than vanilla.

Finally, the villagers know that Max is a giant teddy bear.

He's a friend who will be there for you no matter when or where!

This is how the story ends,

With Max and Pepper, forever the best of friends.

We are all different, including you.

Welcome changes, welcome what's new.

Be kind and understanding of others who are not like you.

Remember, in their eyes, you are pretty different too.

Don't be scared of them, instead smile and be nice.

You might make a new friend after breaking the ice.

Like Max, be proud of who you are,

Kindness and love will get you far.

Try to think first with your heart,

And always say excuse me when you fart.

Like Pepper, no matter how small you are, you have a voice.

How you use it, will always be your choice.

Listen closely to the wind next time you are outside,

It carries Pepper's purr, happy and full of pride.

Let that gentle wind be your guide

To always live life with your heart and mind open wide.

Made in the USA
San Bernardino, CA
21 September 2015